# the BOOK that EATS PEOPLE

by
John Perry

illustrations by
Mark Fearing

TRICYCLE PRESS
Berkeley

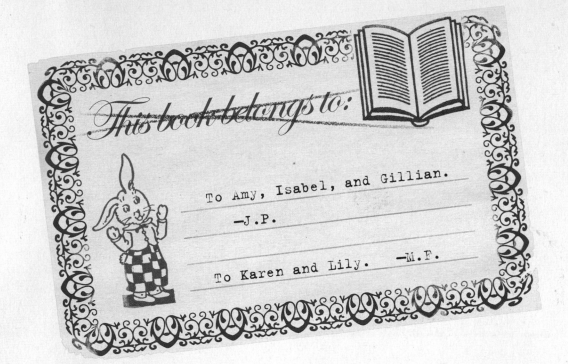

This book belongs to:

To Amy, Isabel, and Gillian.

—J.P.

To Karen and Lily.    —M.F.

# CAUTION!

This is a book that eats people.

If you hear growling while you're reading it, stop reading, close the cover, and put something heavy on top of it.

**DO NOT** let your little brother or sister read this book— especially when it's hungry.

You should always assume this book is hungry.

# Remember:

This is **NOT** a storybook.

It is **NOT** a book of rhymes.

It's a book that eats people.

One day in Little Rock, Arkansas, Sammy Ruskin forgot to wash his hands after lunch, and the book tasted peanut butter on his fingers.

So the book—this book—went SNAP! And took a bite! And then another and another. Sammy squirmed and wriggled. Sammy squealed and yelled. Sammy pulled as hard as he could, but the book ate him. Then it coughed up his bones and they clattered across the floor like wooden blocks.

That was the first person this book ate.

If you hear pages rustling, it's probably because the book smells something yummy. But if you hear a sound like an octopus in a tub of yogurt, that is the book's empty stomach and the book is RAVENOUS. If you hear THAT, find someone nearby—FAST—who might taste delicious to a book.

After this book ate Sammy Ruskin,
his parents gave it to a library,
where it sat trapped and mad,
tightly shelved between *The
Complete Guide to the Saints* and
*Sandwiches Through the Ages*.
Its stomach growled and growled
for weeks until late one evening,
someone left the guide to the saints
on a table in the reference section.

*The Complete Guide To The Saints*

What Happened to Sam Ruskin?

Sandwiches Through the Ages

That night, while the moon shone, the book devoured
*Famous Americans, Who's Who in American Business,*
and Mr. Singh the security guard, who yelled like crazy.

When the librarians came in, it was swallowing the last pages of *How Things Work*.

Titles like *What Happened to Sam Ruskin?* keep some library books shelved forever. So, while the librarians wept, this book traded covers with *All About Dolphins*. And that very same day, right about the time when everybody likes a chocolate-chip cookie, Victoria Glassford checked it out.

She put the book on her nightstand, but before she could finish brushing her teeth, it jumped up, thumped her on the head, and gobbled her down, beginning with her polished pink toenails.

## Have you ever heard a book burp?

*What Happened to Sam Ruskin?*

This is a bad book. A book with teeth and claws. It's a monster that eats people. You should throw it in the fireplace on the coldest February day. You should grind it page by page in your daddy's coffee grinder.

Experts say that when a book eats someone it's either self-defense or a mistake, and the book never eats anyone again.

But this book ate Sammy, Victoria, and Mr. Singh, and then it ate Joey, Juan, and Isabel when they found it in a heap of boxes on a street in Philadelphia.

Judge Cox, who loved all books, sent it to the zoo where zookeepers tried to reform it. They fed it fried chicken, pickles, hot dogs, ice cream, noodles, and toast, but nothing worked because this book craves people. When it chewed through a zookeeper's shoe, they finally gave up and put a label on it that says THE BOOK THAT EATS PEOPLE in big, bold letters.

They took it and locked it in a jail cell, where it
ate Chuck Anderson, who deserved it.

Some people think it's cruel to chain a book.
The guards did it anyway.

Published in the United States by Tricycle Press, an imprint of the
Crown Publishing Group, a division of Random House, Inc., New York.
www.crownpublishing.com
www.tricyclepress.com

Tricycle Press and the Tricycle Press colophon are registered
trademarks of Random House, Inc.

Library of Congress Cataloging-in-Publication Data:

Perry, John, 1967–
The book that eats people / by John Perry ; illustrations by Mark Fearing.
     p. cm.
Summary: The reader is warned to be careful around this book, which has already eaten
several people and is always hungry.
[1. Books—Fiction.]  I. Fearing, Mark, ill. II. Title.
PZ7.P4388Bo 2009
[E]—dc22

2008042393

ISBN 978-1-58246-268-4

Printed in China

Design by Betsy Stromberg
Typeset in Trade Gothic
The art in this book was rendered in Photoshop and incorporates
collage elements.

2 3 4 5 6 7 — 14 13 12 11 10

First Edition

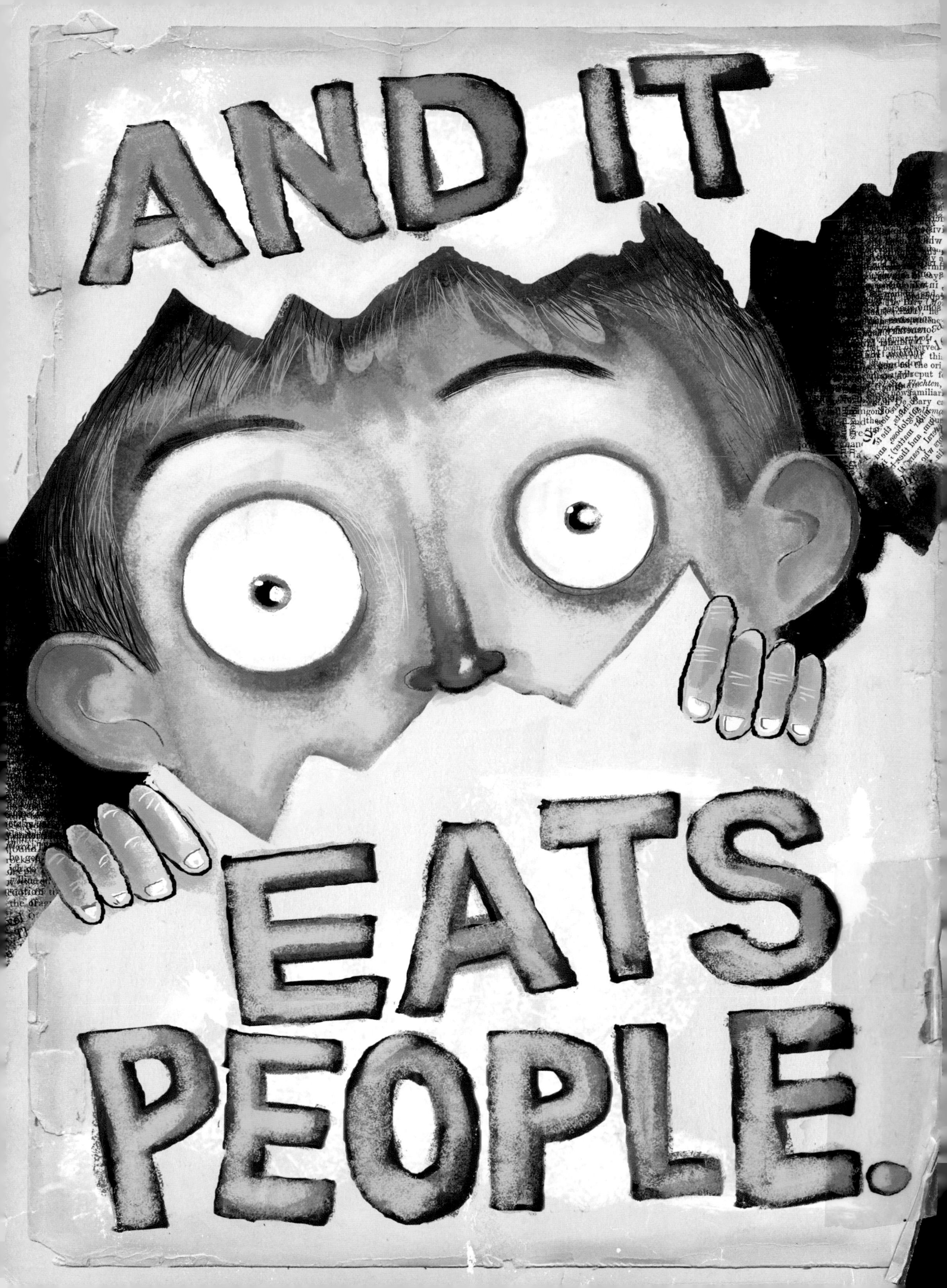
AND IT
EATS
PEOPLE.

So now everyone knows what kind of book this is.
Who knows where YOU found it. But be careful.

Never read this book with syrupy fingers.

Never read it with cookies in your pocket.

Never turn your back on it.

Never NEVER EVER read this book alone.

# Because this book is
# ALWAYS hungry.